W9-BIE-997

WELCOME TO
PASSPORT TO READING
A beginning reader's ticket to a brand-new world!

Every book in this program is designed to build read-along and read-alone skills, level by level, through engaging and enriching stories. As the reader turns each page, he or she will become more confident with new vocabulary, sight words, and comprehension.

These PASSPORT TO READING levels will help you choose the perfect book for every reader.

READING TOGETHER
Read short words in simple sentence structures together to begin a reader's journey.

READING OUT LOUD
Encourage developing readers to sound out words in more complex stories with simple vocabulary.

READING INDEPENDENTLY
Newly independent readers gain confidence reading more complex sentences with higher word counts.

READY TO READ MORE
Readers prepare for chapter books with fewer illustrations and longer paragraphs.

This book features sight words from the educator-supported Dolch Sight Words List. This encourages the reader to recognize commonly used vocabulary words, increasing reading speed and fluency.

For more information, please visit passporttoreadingbooks.com.

Enjoy the journey!

Hachette Book Group supports the right to free expression and the value of copyright. The purpose of copyright is to encourage writers and artists to produce the creative works that enrich our culture.

The scanning, uploading, and distribution of this book without permission is a theft of the author's intellectual property. If you would like permission to use material from the book (other than for review purposes), please contact permissions@hbgusa.com. Thank you for your support of the author's rights.

Little, Brown and Company
Hachette Book Group
1290 Avenue of the Americas, New York, NY 10104
Visit us at LBYR.com

First Edition: June 2018

Little, Brown and Company is a division of Hachette Book Group, Inc. The Little, Brown name and logo are trademarks of Hachette Book Group, Inc.

The publisher is not responsible for websites (or their content) that are not owned by the publisher.

ISBNs: 978-0-316-48035-2 (pbk.), 978-0-316-48033-8 (ebook), 978-0-316-48031-4 (ebook), 978-0-316-48032-1 (ebook)

PRINTED IN THE UNITED STATES OF AMERICA

CW

10 9 8 7 6 5 4 3 2 1

Passport to Reading titles are leveled by independent reviewers applying the standards developed by Irene Fountas and Gay Su Pinnell in *Matching Books to Readers: Using Leveled Books in Guided Reading*, Heinemann, 1999.

MARVEL
ANT-MAN AND THE WASP

Adapted by R.R. Busse
Story by Steve Behling
Illustrated by Ron Lim, Andy Smith,
Davide Mastrolonardo, Pierluigi Cosolino,
and Fabio Paciulli
Directed by Peyton Reed
Produced by Kevin Feige, p.g.a.
Written by Chris McKenna & Erik Sommers
and Paul Rudd & Andrew Barrer & Gabriel Ferrari

Ⓛ Ⓑ
LITTLE, BROWN AND COMPANY
New York   Boston

Attention, ANT-MAN AND THE WASP fans!
Look for these words when you read
this book. Can you spot them all?

villain

teacher

technology

backpack

This is Scott Lang.

Scott loves his daughter, Cassie.
He does good things to make
her proud of him.

He did a bad thing once.

He was just trying to help people,

but Scott went to jail.

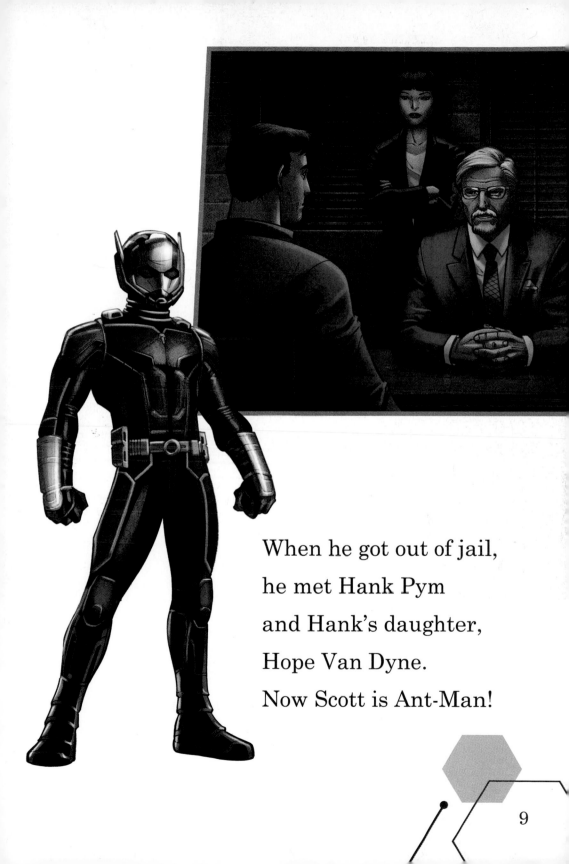

When he got out of jail,
he met Hank Pym
and Hank's daughter,
Hope Van Dyne.
Now Scott is Ant-Man!

Ant-Man is a Super Hero!

He can shrink and talk to ants!

He stops a super villain named Yellowjacket.

Cassie is so proud of her dad!

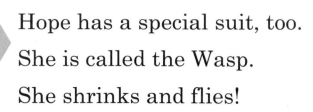

Hope has a special suit, too.
She is called the Wasp.
She shrinks and flies!

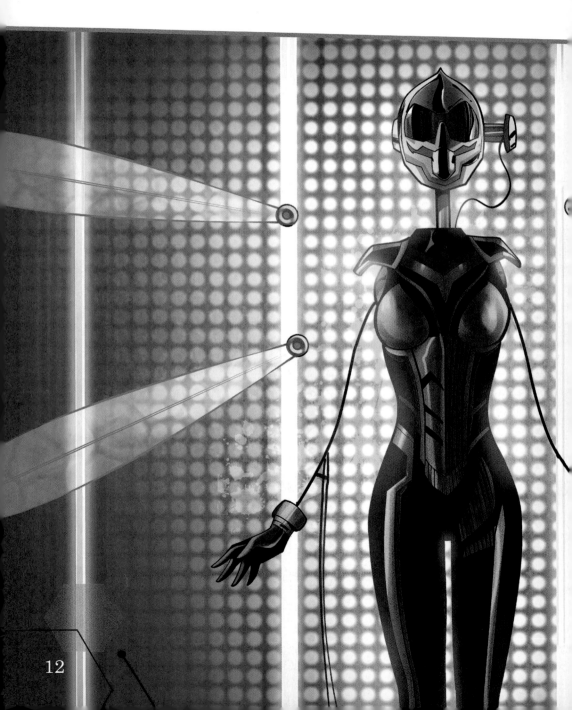

She and Scott work together.

Hope is a great fighter.

Scott and Hope can shrink down
to the size of ants.
An old shrinking suit is missing.

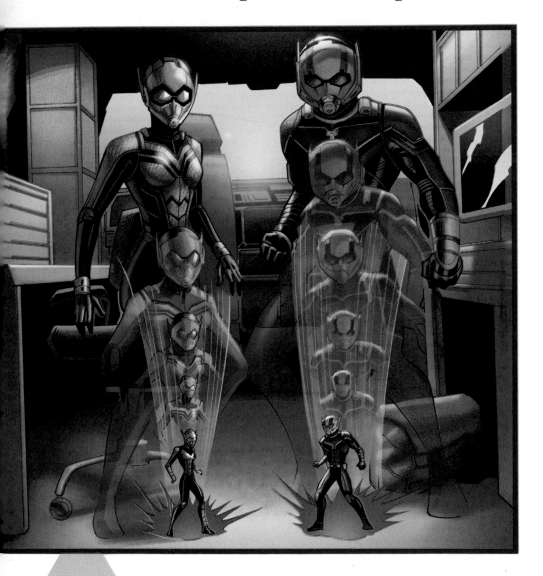

Oops—Cassie takes the suit to school!

"You hid the suit in a trophy?"

Hope asks Scott.

"It seemed smart at the time," he says.

Oh no!

Scott's suit is broken.

He starts to grow!

Hope helps Scott hide
in a broom closet.
Teachers cannot find them.
Super Heroes are not
allowed in schools!

Scott keeps growing!

He is ten feet tall!

Hope tries to fix his suit.

She is very good with technology.

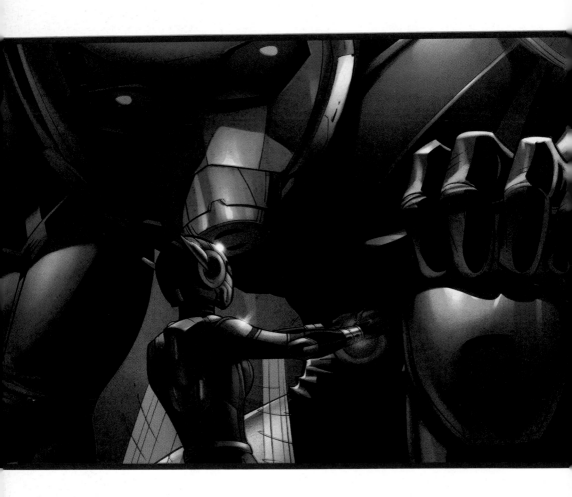

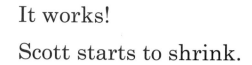

It works!

Scott starts to shrink.

Wait—Scott is still shrinking!
Soon he is only three feet tall.

He finally stops shrinking.

Hope laughs very hard.

Poor Scott.

Scott is very lucky.

There is a lost and found!

Soon Scott finds clothes that fit him.

He looks just like a kid!

"Adorable," Hope says.

"Where is your hall pass?" a teacher asks.

Hope and Scott run away!

They still need to find the missing suit.

They make it to Cassie's classroom.

Scott finds her backpack.

The trophy with the suit in it is inside.

Scott does not want to take the trophy.
Cassie will be sad if it is gone.

Hope finds the suit!

It is taped to the side of the trophy.

Scott watches Cassie play basketball with her friends.

He is so happy to be her dad.
He is sorry they had to sneak
into her school.

Scott and Hope talk about Cassie.
But the teacher finds them!
"Hey! You two!" he yells.

Scott shrinks a little bit more.
Ant-Man and the Wasp
make it past the teacher
and look for the door.

Scott and Hope make it outside!
They have the suit, and Cassie
will finish her day at school.
What adventures will they have next?